MENTAL ELEVATION

TRAVIS GEORGE

Contents

About The Author

Poem 1
Find And Rise!

Why wonder when you're always lost in wonders?
How can you get on top when you're always stuck up under?
It begins with a mentality change,
To begin to change a lot of things.
You may have to reprogram your brain,
Tame the unexplained with the understanding that there's
pain.
Failure rains,
Can be difficult, but success springs from hard work.
Obstacles will lurk, only to insert roadblocks.

They intentionally knock and knock,
Until finally, you get knocked off of the right path.
The enemies in the race, all different sizes and shapes,
Seemingly impossible to interpret the fakes before it's too late,
because time is moving so fast.
Before you know it, you have more problems remaining from
the past.
What's sad is that you add a splash of "Kiss my ass" to answer
your problems, which is so bad, because then all you know is
to crash.
Until you absorb one good blast of sunshine,
Such a beautiful time.
Your mind is no longer blind.

The truth is not hard to find, sometimes, some is not enough
time.
You have your own mind, control when the clock chimes.
With the Lord reunite your bond, because without Him no
meaningful battle is won.
You are the gun, but what good is that if you can't shoot off?
Big mouth with nothing that comes out,
Can't have a home too comfortable with living in a house.

You must get out, put everything in order.
Life span is getting shorter.
Live for your son and your daughter.
Get money, but don't live for a quarter.
What symbolizes real happiness is remaining in peace no matter how bad it gets.
Instead of feeling like a pile of shit that sits, dried with no motive.

A broken compass with no direction,
Lonely with li'l affection.
Every move you choose containing discretion,
Even after sleeping, becoming more restless.
Destroying mind, body, and spirit is what oneself has been investing.
What you put in is what you get out.
Accomplish the goals that you set out.
Do everything from the heart, All of you, not just a part.
Do not only wonder, but have much meaning,
Stay positive to stay away from demons.
If you think everything is bad, then shut up and quit complaining,
Because it's only yourself that you should be blaming.
Paint the pictures that you're framing,
Quit questioning the things that need no explaining.
Get to know yourself for confidence,
Believe in yourself throughout all suffering.

Do this, and you will not get lost in wonders,
No more being stuck up under!

Poem 2
We Are Able!

So many things I have been through,

Had to use my brain while I was into.

Made many mistakes, like we as men do.

Seems like pain is who I'm closest kin to.

So I grab my paper, regroup, and let my pen loose.

Sometimes it's untamed, so don't let me offend you.

Easily can happen with words, no matter what they tended to do.

I'm only defending the truth, to please your ears, I'm not pretending to.

Not just one, but I'm speaking to many of you.

We must change some of these things that we continue to do.

Since the beginning, we've been sinning.

But instead of blending in it, we should begin being more friendly.

Knocking on doors, closer to the ending.

Haven't been repenting, so many charges still pending.

Much death amongst the living.

When there's nothing else, there's forgiveness.

Quit holding grudges, like it's forbidden.

Don't know what to say, shut up and just listen.

Take a break, stop walking, and just envision.

If you do, you can realize how to chew and swallow your pride.

Quit balling it up inside.

Instead of letting your heart get involved, you let ignorance and anger move in to solve.

This triggers dangers to evolve.

Then hate to family, friends, even to strangers you lob.

Yourself from happiness you rob,

Sitting back laughing, but truly you sob.

You are the cob, share with and love the corn around you.

Don't just listen, but suck it up and find truth.

There's only One God, and He resides beside you.

He uses His word to remind us who has All and Everlasting Power.

So Brothers and Sisters, Love Minute By Minute, And Hour After Hour!

Summary: We are all able to forgive, so let's quit holding grudges. Instead, let's build and grow in Unity! Much Love!!

Poem 3
My Maker!

In 1982, she came through just for me,

Sweating and pushing, because it was for me, she was in a rush to see.

Came out as little Travis, long head and very unique.

So high expectations were a must for me to be.

Couldn't yet talk, but was given a breast, so I was ready to eat.

Had pampers, so I didn't have to hold steady to pee.

Cried a whole lot, she grabbed me, and I was headed to sleep.

Warm and loving care was my only real need.

Sensitive heart growing up, so often my feelings would hurt.

Took my problems to you, Lady, you would take them away, didn't know how, but it worked, even when you weren't there, you'd make my way up in church.

Put into the collection plate, from the money that you gave from your purse.

You are a special gift, that was made for this earth.

A strong woman, that knew she had to do it, so never strayed from hard work.

Kids at home, so food into their stomachs, she had to insert.

I was #3, so didn't have to be 1st,

Cuz, I was still held close to that special place, Right up under your shirt.

Never gave up, because you knew, that things could've been worse.

Blew up sometimes, but never did you burst.

33 years old now, and I can say from you, I've learned discipline and respect.

I'm not Stupid, I'm Happy, and not yet met death.

I'm working, I'm trying, and ready for the next step.

I Love You Ma, You Did Great, And Great Is Your Best!

Summary: I will always love You, Mama. No Matter What, You will Always Fill that Special place in My Heart!

PS. I sincerely thank you!

Poem 4
One Love!

It's never easy, only seems to get harder,

Losing someone that you love, sister, brother, mother, or father.

Grandparents, uncles, aunts, and our kids,

No matter who it is, it's always losing a friend.

Everybody gotta go, but I hate losing especially when,

It's out of a selfish act, another brutal attack.

Cowardly using guns, only shooting to react.

To me, it's really stupid to be exact,

Because once you shoot, you cannot take that shot back.

Wishing it wasn't true, but you cannot stop facts.

The fact is, I wish we could stop that,

Killing one another over materials.

Early in the morning, death toll high, even before the pouring of your cereal.

Shots ringing out, but you just might not be hearing them.

But they got somebody, somewhere, with fear in them,

Hoping that don't get hit and that they can just be missed,

Part of a family somewhere, that they will be missed to kiss.

Forced to get through this,

Madness, that continues, but needs to cease to exist.

It's peace that I insist, pains me, pumping hard my fist.

Trying to pound away this suffering, that I just don't get.

Because of the way things are going, it's not the way that I picked.

Another murder, death, kill, has really gotten me pissed,

Destroying another's life, why can't we just resist?

So many broken homes, so this is something that I just can't dismiss.

If I only had one, for peace, I would make this wish,

I would make this senseless killing, a bad habit that we kick.

From hate to love, I would be fast to switch.

It's past time, to quit letting time past while we sit.

We need to find other ways to vibe and vent.

To put the guns down, we need to try to commit.

Because it's together, if we strive for peace, then it will be peace, that we will get!

Summary: We are all roots connected to the same tree, so let's join together as one, so that we all may flourish in peace!

Much Love!

Poem 5
Stand Up and Man Up!

Nobody's a punching bag, punch me, I'm punching back.

I'm only launching facts.

Feeding on drama, what kind of lunch is that?

In everyone else's Kool-Aid, worried about who got laid and who didn't.

If it's not your business, why are you sniffing?

Stand up guy, so why are you tripping?

This is your feminine side standing at attention.

It's gotten my attention, so I'm venting.

I'm asking questions really, 'cause I just don't get it.

Not a part of me, so I just don't feel it.

Where are all of my fellow warriors that's willing to die for the children?

Eye for an eye, even if it's killing.

What about kneeling? Giving respect where respect is due.

A difference between standing up for the ones that never respect you.

That choose to neglect you.

Front row view, to seeing you doing bad, but will never help you.

Why do you go all out for another to accept you?

There's no one that can live for you, except you.

It's better sooner than later to accept truth.

I'm not saying that you should, but what you better do.

Many parts to your body, but I'm calling to the inner you.

Face yourself from the inside, this is an inner feud.

The way you're walking in your shoes, is not very manly.

For who we need right now, you're not being very handy.

Our kids need men that are not sweeter than candy.

The ones that they can see that haven't vanished.

Leaving them feeling abandoned.

The farmer that planted the seeds, not only taking them for granted.

Leaving them all by themselves, forcing them to manage.

It's Now time to make a stand, not a time to panic.

Pick up your big boy drawers and put down your panties.

Been going through this destructive cycle, but now we've got to get around the damage.

We've got to listen to our women to get more understanding.

They're feeling lost, not knowing who to turn to.

To any real man, how can this not concern you?

Destroy but never build, this is what germs do.

Why would you bite the hand that gave birth and even nurtured you?

Disrespecting our women, only expresses the worst of you.

The way that we downgrade them, we're failing the test.

Many zeros, and incompletes.

Why is it with them, do we choose to compete?

We're running the wrong race, losing by many feet.

So much of the wrong energy being released.

With our women, we shouldn't be enemies.

But the one's holding it down, that will stand up and defend with ease.

We have a protective nature in our genes.

If we want to survive, then we gotta put the woman back on top, by any means.

It's necessary to treat her as queen.

No more tug-a-war, let's just meet up as a team.

This is reality, not just made up as a dream.

It's past time to wake up and step up, this is urgent, so I Scream.

We Must Begin, placing our women high, to rightfully accept our place as Kings!

Poem 6
Gotta Keep Pushing

Our past can contain many things,

Some strange and things that we wish we could change,

Some brought pain and there's the ones that left a stain.

Due to bad timing, there's some that we wish we could rearrange.

But no matter what's in the past, leave it in the past, so that your present, never contains the same.

Gotta live in the present and keep pushing forward.

Keep pushing towards, better days.

Can't allow past situations, to keep you in a daze.

It's like running around in circles, stuck in a maze.

Gotta let go, get peace, don't get stuck in a rage.

Life is a whole book, so don't get stuck on a page.

Only flip backwards, if it's truly something that you're ready to tackle.

Gotta face what happened, to truly be able to capture.

Can't control your destiny if you never master.

The things that's holding you down is a natural disaster.

Maybe because your father left, leaving you feeling like a bastard.

So it's with him, you continue holding a grudge.

Forgiveness is cold, knee-deep in the mud.

Weeping every time that you think about all of the missing kisses and hugs.

Wondering did he ever miss you, or did he just shrug?

The thought alone brings about so much hate and disgust.

The way your uncle touched you when you were young, made you grow a hate for love.

So sad, the sexual acts that you were forced to indulge.

Molestation seems to be at an all-time high.

That every thought of mistrust and manipulation makes you want to cry.

Wrongfully feeling guilty, and you just wonder why.

I know your pain, I can't take away but I just wanna try.

I know that you wanted to fly, to escape away from the rape.

Constantly saying "No" but he forced you to take.

I know it seems like it's madness, trying so hard to get past it.

If I could, I would grab every rapist, and beat them bad with a passion.

I want to apologize for them, because I'm so very sorry that it happened.

These are just a few things that I wish I could change.

But since I can't, I'm going to speak out, in hopes, that it never happens again!

If you have ever been through

anything similar in your life, just know

that I'm sending Peace and Power,

So Stay Strong on Your Road to Recovery!

Much Love!

Poem 7
RIP

Death can definitely be a hard pill to swallow.

Here in the flesh today, but missing tomorrow.

When I open up, all I feel is the sorrow.

Not much to focus on, but the happiness that follows.

Memories, so many, do you remember the times?

Old stories made brand new, I'm not so into goodbyes.

Hello to everyone who has ever felt like this in their lives.

Vision a little blurry from the tears in their eyes.

Readily waiting for the pain to go away, condolences accepted but nothing changes,

No matter what they say.

It simply hurts, even knowing that there's no one exempt on this earth.

We all must one day perish,

Back to the dust in which we came, one day all will be buried,

Leaving behind hearts heavy.

Thinking about it ahead of the time can be scary,

But the Truth will set you free.

And the Truth is, that our loved ones live through we,

Between us, the passing of energy.

Close your eyes and open your mind, and it will be them, that you will see!

To All The ones That We Love And Miss,

May They Rest In Power!

Much Love!

17

Poem 8
God's Grace

To begin to be free, you gotta truly want to be.

Everything may not go as you planned, but God is working in your favor, you gotta believe.

Blind faith is more apparent than the eyes can see,

Because it's God's Greatest Promise, and it's for you and for me.

When things seem rough, don't let go, but hold on tighter.

Made to be strong on these bumpy roads, 'cause you are a fighter.

Continue lifting the heavy loads, and they will become lighter road.

The sun is shining at the end of the road, once you get through the fire.

The devil is a liar, because we shall overcome.

Stand face to face with adversities, do not fear and don't run.

Keep your eyes on the prize, because we are blessed beyond measures.

Made in God's image, so never see yourself as lesser.

Pain doesn't last always, so just know that it will subside.

And death is not the end of life, but only the gateway to how We Truly Survive!

Poem 9
Purpose

Open the blinds and search behind the curtains.

Hopefully in due time, we all find that we all have a purpose.

We're all here because we have a reason to live.

Some are closer than others, with the understanding of what that reason is.

Do you even have a clue what you're here to do?

If you do, are you following it through, or is it just following you?

Waiting for you grab it and take action.

Not to neglect it, you gotta accept it, to make it happen.

Attach with it passion, always keep it, and never pass it.

Make it be that every day of the week is everlasting.

Are you here to change the world, make life better for every boy and every girl?

Maybe your purpose is to sing, beautiful songs for many ears to ring.

Have you been called to write, words that can rise the dead to life?

Are you here to fight, to join with the ones that stand up for what's right?

You might be here to be a mentor, to help another understand what their life is meant for.

You might be a speaker with a strong voice, to speak up for the weak, when theirs seem hoarse.

Maybe your gift is to dance, to entertain and attract millions of fans.

No matter who you are, there's a reason that you're on this surface.

So Dig Deep, Reach Inside Yourself, And Pull Out, What Is Your Purpose!

Poem 10
Glory Be To God!

I thank you, God, for my strength.
It's because of you, every day, my head, I am able to lift.
Without your mercy, I couldn't even exist.
Away from your love, I will never resist.
Can't let go, never will I dismiss.
To speak of your mercy to the world, I will take any risk.
I won't fake, nor will I flinch.
I'm with you, so no weapon formed against me shall prosper.
Because nothing possibly can stop you.
You take away all of my problems.
Helping me to hop over every obstacle.
You turn my stormy days and nights, tropical.
I'm so glad that I got you.
I'm going to bring back memories, to all of the ones,
That seem like they forgot you.
Not really understanding how could they.
You're the highlight of every good day.
All things are only possible, through your good grace.
So, I just would love to say, thank you, because
It's exactly what I should say.
Amen!

Poem 11
Killing Our Kids!

Babies having babies and kids are killing kids,
So many children taken early, it's so crazy how we live.
Babies having babies and kids are killing kids,
So many children taken early, it's so crazy how we live.

Babies having babies is crazy, not mature enough
To even raise themselves,
Knowing nothing about being responsible, they themselves,
Stay searching for help.

Many are selfishly dropping seeds, without the thought
Of the effects.
Why bring another life into this world, when it's their own
Lives they regret?

Age ain't nothing but a number, what's more important,
Is the respect.
What's sad is, the more that they grow, there's even more
Trash, that they accept.

Taught that killing is cool, so very soon, taking away
Another's life.
So backwards, the way that they are learning, what is
Obviously wrong, they think that it is right.

Guided by parents that are apparently,
Still wet behind the ears.
Foolishly following the nonsense, that becomes
Set throughout the years.

This destructive cycle is one, that I really wish
Would disappear.

But until it does, there will be many more families,
That will shed so many tears!

Poem 12
My Choice

I must play my position, many choices and decisions.

Gotta pay close attention, or risk falling victim to clouded vision.

Wrong move could lead to falling in an instant.

Acknowledging the difference between, from what is and what isn't.

Gotta be man enough not to allow my emotions to rule.

Staying away from the heat, by not feeding fire to the fuel.

Me against the world is the duel, and I'm determined to win.

Didn't arrive here by luck, it was on purpose that

I was sent.

So me putting in, is worth my every cent.

Taking every risk that is needed.

Because if I'm not giving my all, it's only myself that

I am cheating.

And everyone around that loves and needs me.

I must believe in, and I must believe me.

I have so many reasons for me to succeed.

To keep from falling into drama, I gotta take heed.

Sometimes, I gotta retreat from the fights, that's not

Worth my muscles flexing.

Knowing right from wrong, so I shouldn't be second-guessing.

Being human, so sometimes, I'm the messenger, that

Ignores his own message.

Satan has a way of bearing a strong presence.

Not my true essence, because he's teaching the wrong lessons.

If I let him, he'll help weaken my strong blessings.

One wrong move, what's been built, can be destroyed in a second.

This is one thing that I know, and I know that I know better.

Stepping up to the plate, because I know that I'm a go-getter.

So my choice is to Show Love, and that is from Now,

Until Forever!

Poem 13
Fight to Unite!

Either We Choose Unity, or It Will Be the

End of You and Me!

It will be the end, no pretend.

No more human race, no more men.

We must comprehend that working together is our only chance.

If not, we're dancing with doom,

Taking away any chance that we have to resume.

Leaving no room, only reasons why we had to go so soon.

Destroying mother earth and her womb,

So much pollution, leaving even less solutions.

Future death and destruction can be the only conclusion.

Through technology we're winning, but overall we're losing.

So many facts that we're refusing,

Leading to the power that we're abusing.

It's like we're killing ourselves just for the amusement.

But I'm not amused with

Dying every day, brother after brother,

Tears falling from the eyes of so many mourning mothers.

I write this today because I see that we're in trouble,

And I really do love you.

So let's unite today and fight to stand with one another!

Poem 14
Thank You!

You are the sun that shines on me when it's a gloomy day.
You are the knees that I kneel on when I get down to pray.
You are the road that I travel, that helps me find my way.
When I need to reflect, I look in the mirror, and you are my
face.
Whenever I cross the finish line, you are my 1st place.
The reason I even cross the line is because you are my race.
Whenever I'm overwhelmed by work, you are my break.
Because you fill me with so much love, I stay away from hate.
With me, you're always true, never are you fake.
Whenever I'm down, you're always on time, never are you late.
Whenever the enemy comes around, you keep me safe.
My foundation above ground, you are my base.
When my feet get weary, you're the reason that I tighten my
lace.
Whether you do or don't know who you are, I just want
To take this time to say,
Thank you!

Poem 15
Priceless!

Strong bond between father and son,

You can feel the pain deep inside if he's fatherless one.

Powerless since the first day that he was born,

Daddy never around to help lessen his mourns.

To teach him why when getting older, every lesson keeps growing,

Everything is a lesson, so it's better to know it.

If you love him, don't hide the love; it's always better to show it.

If this is a wound that needs to be healed, be a man and sew it.

For a special purpose in life, every child is chosen,

Learning to become a master, because they already be glowing.

Early since birth, juices already flowing,

Ready to begin pouring all over this earth.

Any father missing his son should search,

Because there's no ego and pride that can ever

Amount to his worth!

Poem 16
I Love You Deuce!

When I think about you, son, it brings me so much joy.
Love and my light, you are my boy.
Not just part of my heart, you are my ending and the start.
Everything in the middle and so much more.
I reminisce thinking about giving you your first bath,
The way you laughed when the water splashed.
Tight grip, you held on to dad with such a mighty grasp.
Was looking forward to every moment that would come after
that.
It's a forever fact that you being born would definitely be one
of my greatest moments.
There's nothing more than I could've asked for,
Simply a blessing that God sent to me for sure.
You are the cure that relieves my stress.
My little prince, you're awesome, and nothing less.
You're like my twin brother, the way that we connect.
And I Will Be Here For You Forever, And This Is
Definitely Something That I Hope You Never Forget!!

Strong bond between father and son,
You can feel the pain deep inside if he's a fatherless one.
Powerless since the first day that he was born,
Daddy never around to help lessen his mourns.
To teach him why when getting older, every lesson keeps
growing,
Everything is a lesson, so it's better to know it.
If you love him, don't hide the love; it's always better to show
it.
If this is a wound that needs to be healed, be a man and sew it.
For a special purpose in life, every child is chosen.
Learning to become a master, because they already be glowing.
Early since birth, juices already flowing.

Ready to begin pouring all over this earth.
Any father missing his son should search,
Because there's no ego and pride that can ever
Amount to his worth!

Dedicated to my son, Travis Terell George II,
AKA Deuce.
Your father will always love you!

Poem 17
Why!

Why does the judge already see you as guilty?

Raped of your innocence, even before your chance to speak.

Why did mom and dad leave you before your birth?

All of the arguing and fighting, while all along you hurt.

Why did you go so many days without food?

Instead of feeding your tummy, they fed their feet, with all of the brand new shoes.

Why does it seem like the sun never shines?

So much drama from the storms that occupy the mind.

Why didn't anyone come to help when you were being molested?

Because they were silent cries for help, so no one heard the message.

And why when you did speak up, still no one seemed to hear?

Maybe they didn't believe you, or chose to hide behind fear.

Why do we choose to hate, instead of aiming to understand?

Indulging prejudice and racism, against our own fellow man.

Why do we fight against what is naturally true?

All of the love, that should be spread between me and you.

Why are we born to live, but many are just living to die?

Because we all have a purpose in life, but to fulfill it, many simply refuse to try.

Why can't we all see eye to eye and face to face?

We can, once we recognize that we're together,

One Love, One Family,

All a Part of the Same Human Race!

Poem 18
Be a Great Example!

Life is a rollercoaster with many dips and turns.
If you get too close to the heat, you will get burned.
So many lessons that are meant for you to learn.
Just because you don't care, doesn't mean that you shouldn't
be concerned.

This earth is infected with many different snakes and worms.
One bite is all it takes to be injected with poisonous germs.
Just trying to get by, many wiggle and squirm,
Barely making it, only slipping through the cracks.
Leeching off of others who work hard, breaking backs.

Some people intentionally place obstacles to try and get you
knocked off track.
They manipulate the truth, teaching false information as facts.
In fact, purpose is more important than popularity or false
power,
And anyone who bullies the weak should be considered a
coward.

Do not become a zombie who only follows the crowd.
Be a leader that helps another soar past the clouds,
Showing our kids who and what they are, so that they can
always be proud,
Teaching them how to be aware of the enemy because there
are many that prowl.

Some can't be tamed, only born to be wild,
Filthy as can be, so foul.
A terrible death should follow anyone who rapes a child.
We are all free to choose, but not free from consequences.
Every action has a reaction, there are no exemptions.

So be careful how you use the tongue, because with it, you can speak life or death.
You should cohabitate positively with others in the world because you're not here to only care for self.
But you are matter that matters, so make sure that your presence is felt,
Because in the end, GOD will judge your heart when nothing else is left!

Poem 19
Behind the Tears!

Behind every tear, there's a story that may have never been told
With every drop comes a pouring, burning deep in the soul.

No matter man, woman, or child, inside, there's a pain that we hold.

A bond that we all share, that actually may be the same when it's disclosed.

Somewhere, someone cries from becoming a rape victim.

The tears flow alone because they feel as if there's no one that will listen.

Behind the tears, there's a child acting out at this very minute,

Feeling abandoned because his or her parents were always missing.

Too busy, pushed away, or wrongly forced to be distant.

It happens way too often, and many times, the reason is simply senseless.

Because of cowardly bullies, there's a release of many tears that flow,

And the bullies are hurt themselves, so they pretend strength, in hopes that nobody knows.

The rumbling from empty stomachs also keeps tears on a steady stream,

Stepped on, stepped over, and neglected, as if the pain was never seen.

Sometimes, an open ear to hear the tears is all that one really needs,

Because Behind Every Tear, There's A Story, That We All Should Take More Time To Read!

Much Love!

Poem 20
No Fear!

What is it that you fear? Do you fear life itself?

Do you fear living life because there's death?

Do you fear being who you truly are, settling for less, only subpar?

Do you fear a loving relationship, pushing away a good mate from the beginning, calling it quits?

Do you fear love, never truly giving it a chance for the lack of trust?

Do you fear driving, never grabbing the wheel, only riding and surviving?

Do you fear being a parent, controlling over the kids, but never do you understand them?

Do you fear church, scared to see inside yourself, because the real truth hurts?

Do you fear school, afraid of knowledge, rather accept being a fool?

Do you fear the truth, rather entertain gossip about who's talking about who?

Do you fear bullies, never standing up to them, always feeling like you couldn't?

Do you fear jail? There are many lessons to be learned even being inside of there.

So ask yourself, what is it that you fear?

I hope it's nothing, because fear is only false evidence appearing real!

Poem 21
BOO WHO?

Boo, I really miss you and will never forget you.
You're planted in my heart, so it's so close, you will forever stick to.
I don't know why I didn't get to "supposedly" tell you goodbye,
Because you're such wonderful energy that I still see, and I know that you will never die.
I can't even lie, there are some things I wish would have gone differently,
But being as stubborn as you are, I knew that you wouldn't even listen.
At night when I close my eyes, I still see you so clearly in my vision.
The presence that you were, and still are, is nothing less than terrific.
So many things that you told and showed me, that really helped me grow.
You told me that "I'm Here For A Purpose," and that the world should know.
It was you who gave me strength during some of my weakest points.
If I even thought about giving up, then it would be me that you would punch.
You stood up and fought some of my bullies back in the day.
You explained to me how things were, no sugar coating, always straight, face to face.
You said "that if I don't stand up for myself, the world would eat me up and swallow."
These are the words that still to this day, I take great heed to and follow.
You told me, "to live for today, because who really knows if there's tomorrow."

I could give up right now, because inside, I'm filled with so
much sorrow.
But it's not what you would want me to do, so I'm not going to
even bother.
And besides, your nephews are depending on me, because I
am their loving father.
I love the way that you bloomed, just like the perfect flower.
And about you, I could sit here and continue writing hour after
hour.
But instead, I'm going to close my eyes and come talk with
you.
Just thought that I would take out a little time, to let them
know, who is BOO!

You are my special friend and
Brother, and I will always love you
Exactly like none other!
RIP
Rest In Power!

Poem 22
Fallen State

It's such a tragedy and blasphemy, how we speak of God more, but express God less.

There are so many Godless things that I've just gotta address.

First of all, I believe that true love conquers all,

But it's this love for destruction that's digging us deeper to fall.

Division is the effect, from what all this evil has caused,

Teaching us lies and deceit, even before we're able to crawl.

The creation of family feuds is making it so unstable to call.

Criticism and judgment are the miscommunication, even before we're able to talk.

It's sickening that the pedophiles with money can get away under this society's law.

An injustice that we should stand against, as if it is the last straw.

What we face is a spiritual battle, and it is evil that is clearly on the rise.

That's why it's impossible for me not to speak up and keep these feelings bottled up inside.

The media is corrupt, so when we watch, what we soak up is the lies.

But it's the truth in plain sight that they hide.

I believe in loving who you want, but onto the masses, homosexuality should not be forced upon.

If it's got to be forced, then natural is not the added up sum.

I'm disappointed in many churches because for the money, on this subject, they refuse to speak.

I believe in come as you are, but how you are should not subject me to be weak.

Popular opinion is not my concern because to reach the promised land, these mountains that we have to climb are steep.

And it's due to this love for life, I've been in it from the beginning.

So until it ends, I will not surrender, nor will I retreat!

Poem 23
Do It For The Kids!

I'm not rapping, only reacting to actions that are actually happening.

Kids torn between mommies and daddies, is naturally tragic.

To be exact, it's madness, and savagely a bad habit.

How did we pass compassion? It's definitely a hurtful question, but I'm asking.

Like the Hulk, it's all this hurt and pain, I really want to smash it.

Because working together, what we can create, is magic.

The taking away of sadness, so that our kids can be laughing.

This is a much needed want, that they want badly.

So mommy and daddy, should get together today, to make sure that they have it!

Poem 24
I Rise!

Another day alive, born again and able to rise.
To forgive the ones that gave me lies, and to stray
from the things that My Lord despises.
I rise to face old fears that I see and still hear,
The ones that show face and still bring me to tears.
The ones that I want to go away but continue to hold on,
That beat me down when I'm weak, when all I wanted was
to be strong.
I rise, to change those things now, that I yearned to change
before.
Always held the keys, but too afraid to open the door.
I rise, to defeat the pain that aims to tarnish my name,
And to destroy the hurt, the guilt, and all of my shame.
I rise, to pass on the love that I've been given,
Sharing with all that will receive, while I'm alive to give it.
I rise, to break free from the chains that hold me back,
So that I can utilize the wings that I know are attached.
I rise, to expose all skeletons that hide in the closet,
Forcing me to grow tired and even more exhausted.
I rise, to be as different as I am, which is extraordinarily
unique,
To not pretend to be another, but totally in love with me.
I rise, to give all Glory to God and His Untouchable Grace.
I just want to say thank you," for allowing me to Rise,
and to live and see another Beautiful Day.
I Smile And I Rise!

Poem 25
Who Cares?

Who cares that you feel the way that you do,

Growing in age, but still never grew.

Who cares if you never have a care, always searching

for something but nothing's ever there.

Who cares to give something when you're searching for

something to wear?

People would rather see you are, but love is definitely

something lovely to share.

Who cares to give an umbrella when feeling the rain?

Who cares enough to be the cure, when all you feel is the pain?

What about when you're feeling insane?

Who cares enough to tell you that you have the will to change?

So many tools that you can use, but you only choose to blame.

Who cares enough to explain all of the rules to the game?

Doing what they do, never because of what you can do

in exchange.

Who cares to listen to you, when you have the blues and
complain?

Do they even care about the drugs that you use to soothe the
brain?

What about the whips and chains, do anybody care that they took your name?

Who cares how you look as long as how you look is strange?

They only care to book you when you shuck and jive the same.

Who cares if you never live, only strive to die for fame?

Character means nothing as long as you survive and maintain.

Many people ride drama just to hide their shame.

You can be on fire, but who cares enough to realize your flame?

Complicating things in our lives that's plain.

Committing suicide, mistaking it for a rise to gain.

Our kids are being hit because of how we drive in our lanes.

Who cares if we deliver destruction to the youth,

as long as you're entertained, caring less about the truth?

Who cares if there's some screws loose, so many never having a clue?

We should all care because we're in this together.

So who cares, I care, and I hope that you do too!

Poem 26
Peace Love and Light

What does it feel like?
I know it doesn't feel right
When you're seeking peace, but they push you to still fight
I'm human, so I still might
Lose myself to the point where I don't really feel nice
When I write, I'm ignited by real life
The fire through my words burn, so you can hear what it feels
like
When you have a vision, there are many that will try to steal
your sight
It's even when you're facing the darkness, gotta still be bright
I know you hate the bills, when they're threatening to kill the
lights
All by yourself, who really knows how you feel tonight?
Every road being traveled is like a bridge filled with ice
Got to move with caution, be careful who you listen to,
because many are rude when they're talking
Fake news is exhausting, when gossiping about him or she,
I don't choose to hear about it
The way that people spread lies, I have a reason to doubt it
While they're searching for drama, I just be seeking in silence
Silent, keeping a breach in the violence
It's ticking every day, so I'm sticking with timing
Tell me, how do you mind it? Kids' stomachs are growling for
food, but can't find it
A contract for selling your soul, why would you sign it?
Why waste so much of it, but wonder where the time went?
So much time spent, on things that amount to nothing
Got to separate the cons from the pros and always amount to
something
Something is always nothing without some substance
Lower self, got to rise above it

Getting you out of character, many smile because they love it
Seeing that you're not priced high, but living your life on a
budget
Knee-deep in it, so it's alright to get muddy
But getting down and dirty shouldn't be a right to be ugly
I don't feed off enemies, I just like to be buddies
Because I speak what I eat, turn out to be touchy subjects
Seeing the drama beforehand, learning how to duck it
The way they treat you privately, but differently in public
When I'm writing, all I'm sniffing out are the subjects
The ones that have you taking takes, and even doubling
There are many things that are troubling,
like getting beat on, but back showing love again
How he reacts, only being smacked by another hand
Loving how it hurts, so you backtrack, and give another chance
Kids seeing how you're hit, so it's their understanding of the
Mother Land
The way they have been taught, growing up without another
plan
Only to step on another is their only stand
Quick to fall for anything on demand
I demand to make a stand before my last dance
When standing at times, I feel like the last man
On my journey, I pass peace and happiness in the trashcan
So I take it out, adding it to my life to make it count
When it seems it's a standstill, I make it bounce
When it dribbles from my pores, I drink every ounce
No matter what I go through, it never lets me down
only lifts me up, so from me to you, this is what I'm giving up
Peace, Love, and Light, this is the life, so it's together,
We Should Just Live It Up!

Poem 27
Can You Hear Me!

Is it time or has time passed?
For you to live in your present, and no longer behind in your
past,
Time is moving so fast,
How would you choose to use it, if you knew that you were
losing your last?

Two and two go together when doing the math,
Instead of complaining, what are you doing to laugh?
Why is it that when you've got it good, you always ruin it with
bad?
Holding on to the wheel, but quickly losing your grasp.

Time is ticking, so you still have time to reflect on all the
things that are missing,
When it comes to holding grudges, are you real vicious?
Always on fire, have you been burning bridges?
Keeping no one close, everyone at a distance.

When the truth is being told, do you even want to listen?
They say, "nothing is free," so why not pay attention?
If you're missing your kids, why not pay them a visit?
Don't take my word for it, just be happy you did it.

All because you've been there before, don't go backwards to
prison,
Mistakes made before, don't go back to those feelings,
Backstabbers can only stab who is willing,
The pain makes you stronger, that's if it don't kill you.

Overwhelming at times, believe me, I feel you,

Gotta stop blaming others for your problems because the
problem is you,
The only way to solve them is to acknowledge the truth,
If you're wrong, say you're wrong, and let the apologies loose.

False character, pride, and ego find a way to reduce,
If you fall, get back up, and find a way to recoup,
Even when hit below the belt, try your best to not stoop,
Please put the guns down, you don't got to shoot.

Just got to learn how to hula-hoop through the loops,
Be a leader, don't just be part of a group,
To reach your full potential, I'll give you a startup, a boost,
No need for beef, only peace, so I'm calling a truce.

Because time is running out, so pick up, because who
I'm calling is you!
Can you hear me?

Poem 28
Do It Now!

When you awake, you can hear the rain as it pounds the
sidewalk,
Many people look you straight in the face but side talk,
I'll accept the blame, it's all my fault,
It's in your shoes, I try to walk,
All the pain that you feel, I try to walk it out,
Listen while I talk about the many things that hit home, so I'm
not talking soft,
Starting with the kids that are stuck in the middle, because
they're kinda caught,
So much time is lost, waiting too late before we find this out,
Searching many paths before they find the route,
The one that they can travel without a reasonable doubt,
To take away the pain from all of the things that they were
forced to see in the house,
Waking up from nightmares, many nights, screaming out,
So many tears used to pour, now it's seeming like a drought,
Streets are not all sesame, so what's clinging is the Grouch,
It's drugs that they realize they can sling from the couch,
Making money because many people put many different things
in their mouths,
Daughter sadly thinking that it's important to swing her
blouse,
Told to "Get That Money" but never taught about seeing the
cost,
Schools teach to be hard workers but nothing about being The
Boss,
Because of how the roads intersect, we always be in a cross,
With each other, so many foolish reasons that we fought,
Relationships, so many choose to season with salt,
Should be real with your spouse because the cheaters get
caught,

Now your partner don't want to hear the things that you speak from your mouth,
Secrets are flossed, everything that's been built, secretly tossed,
One wrong move can make things merely a thought,
Out of the door, all it takes is clearly a walk,
This is when the feelings get lost,
Give me a second, allow me to quickly enter then get out,
Women want time, men want time, kids want time, but it's this time together, neither can find,
Love pushing to spread, but only being confined,
Time only showing beings, pushing around,
Loving each other, but ignoring one another,
In it together, but not exploring like a couple,
So many things to accomplish in so little time,
Moving faster every day with no intentions of slowing down,
There's many things that we wouldn't have went through if we knew what we know right now,
Everything happens for a reason, can't change them, so it's about what we can do right now,
We hold the keys to our present, to open up a future full of beautiful blessings,
These tools, if we don't use, we will lose and regret it,
This is our life to live, and our choice, whether we choose to edit,
That's why I choose to spread love, so no matter what day it is,
I hope that you never ever forget it!
Much Love!

Poem 29
What She Wants and What She Needs!

She knows what she wants and what she needs,

She wants a strong man that's willing to lead,

One that won't hesitate to tend to her needs,

Exploring her fantasies, and go the extra mile to make sure
that she's pleased.

She wants a man that will make a stand,

One that thinks ahead, instead of waiting to plan,

She needs a fighter, but also a friend,

She needs a man that will battle her problems, but also
comprehend.

She needs a man that will help her to grow,

Not a "Yes Man", but one who's not afraid to say No,

Not one who talks a good game, but never do he show,

She wants a man that's not afraid to let his love flow.

She needs one who's powerful enough to be sensitive,

Real Love, not only one for pretend,

She wants a man that she can talk to,

Not one that treats her desires like a walk-thru.

She needs one that will give her credit, when to her, the credit is all due,

Not one that mistreats her feelings, but treats her feeling brand new,

She wants a man that's like her air to breathe,

She needs one that will stay, and not just up and leave.

In one that she can always trust, that won't ever deceive,

These are the things that All Real Women Want,

And What They Definitely Need.

Poem 30
I'm Being Kept Away!

I know that you came into this world without your Dad, and
it's sad,
Can't even be around to make you laugh, makes me mad,
Gotta keep my focus on the future, and not the past,
Because whenever I think about you in my mind, I feel it
crash.

Into my heart, feeling hurt by how we are torn apart,
Relations with a married woman, maybe it was wrong from the
start,
I never intended to be away, and leave you alone in the dark,
But now I'm dealing with this issue, hurting so bad, has gotten
me feeling for the tissue.

My son who I love, but missing, Is You,
Tried talking to your mother, made multiple calls to get
through,
She always hung up the phone, and pretty much gave me the
boot,
Left me stuck in a maze, Lost, only with the wonders of
wondering, what is it exactly that I should do.

She told me, "Not to call back, and for her number to lose,"
Many evil thoughts of showing out, like I had nothing to lose,
For my son, it's a choice, that I was jumping to choose,
Already feeling haunted with the blues.

Allowing a man to raise my son that doesn't have a clue,
What is it that you love, and the things that you will do?
What turns you on and the things what will make your blood
boil?
Honestly son, what I wanted for you, was more.

I know that you are going to fly, so I just wanted to be there to
explore when you soar,
Calm you down when you roar,
My life is full of blessings, and you're definitely one of the
number ones in store,
I know that you can't hear me, but I hope that you can feel me
for sure.

Daddy Loves You, and I Miss You, Hope You Can Feel It,
Because The Feeling Is Pure!

Dedicated to my son, Jacob Smith
AKA Jacob George
Daddy Will Always Love You